The Kingdom of Wrenly

9

The Bard and the Beast

By Jordan Quinn

Illustrated by Robert McPhillips

LITTLE SIMON

New York London Toronto Sydney New Delhi

LITTLE SIMON

An imprint of Simon & Schuster Children's Publishing Division
1230 Avenue of the Americas, New York, New York 10020
First Little Simon paperback edition November 2015
Copyright © 2015 by Simon & Schuster, Inc.
Also available in a Little Simon hardcover edition.
All rights reserved, including the right of reproduction in whole or in part in any form.
LITTLE SIMON is a registered trademark of Simon & Schuster, Inc., and associated colophon is a trademark of Simon & Schuster, Inc.
For information about special discounts for bulk purchases, please contact Simon & Schuster Special Sales at 1-866-506-1949 or business@simonandschuster.com.
The Simon & Schuster Speakers Bureau can bring authors to your live event. For more information or to book an event contact the Simon & Schuster Speakers Bureau at 1-866-248-3049 or visit our website at www.simonspeakers.com.
Manufactured in the United States of America 0418 MTN
6 8 10 9 7
Library of Congress Cataloging-in-Publication Data
Quinn, Jordan.
The bard and the beast / by Jordan Quinn ; illustrated by Robert McPhillips.
pages cm. — (The kingdom of Wrenly ; 9)
Summary: Prince Lucas would rather be enjoying the outdoors with his best friend, Clara, than learning to play the lute, until a visiting bard demonstrates the power of music.
ISBN 978-1-4814-4397-5 (hc) — ISBN 978-1-4814-4396-8 (pbk) — ISBN 978-1-4814-4398-2 (eBook)
[1. Princes— Fiction. 2. Bards and bardism— Fiction. 3. Music— Fiction. 4. Basilisks (Mythical animals)— Fiction.] I. Title.
PZ7.Q31945Bar 2015
[Fic]— dc23
2015000423

CONTENTS

CHAPTER 1

Music Lessons

"Yes! Sir Archie won!" Prince Lucas shouted.

"No, Sir Fred won!" cried Clara.

"Squawk!" crowed Ruskin, Lucas's pet dragon. He was definitely on the prince's side.

"Okay, let's call it a *tie!*" Lucas said.

"No way!" argued Clara. "Sir Fred won fair and square!"

Prince Lucas and his best friend, Clara, had just had a toad race. They argued and laughed as they ran down the castle halls.

Then, all at once, Lucas's muddy leather boots skidded to a stop. Clara didn't see in time and bumped into Lucas. Ruskin smacked into the back of Clara's knees. Queen Tasha blocked the hallway. She tapped her black velvet shoe on the stone floor and stared disapprovingly at the mud-covered children.

"Where on earth have you been, Lucas?" she said sternly. "You are

late for your first music lesson!"

Clara peeked out from behind Lucas. "Um, I'd better be going," she said uncomfortably. Then she turned and hurried toward the door.

The queen kept her eyes on her son. Lucas wiped some toad slime on his pants and sighed heavily.

"Come on, Mother," he complained. "You

know I don't want to play a musical instrument!"

"It's not up for discussion," his mother said. "Music is part of your royal education."

Then she grabbed Lucas by the hand and marched him to the music room.

Lucas stumbled along behind his mother.

Master Aldrich, the royal music teacher, greeted them at the door. He had dark shoulder-length hair, a pointy nose, and a swirly mustache. He bowed to the queen. She nodded and left the room. Then Master Aldrich slid his glasses to the bridge of his nose and glared over them.

"You're tardy," he declared as if Lucas didn't know. The

teacher sniffed. "Well then," he went on, "shall we pick an instrument?"

Master Aldrich walked—rather like a duck—across the room and sat down with a floating golden harp. The instrument hovered in the air as the music teacher began to pluck the strings with his long, skinny fingers.

"Heavenly, isn't it?" he said.

Lucas shrugged. "Too many strings for my taste," he said.

Master Aldrich got up and pulled a recorder from a shelf. "Here's a simple instrument that's easy to learn," he said, putting the pipe to his lips.

Lucas watched his teacher's fingers cover and uncover the holes on the recorder as he played a short tune.

"Well?" Master Aldrich said, looking at the prince.

"Too many holes," Lucas replied.

Master Aldrich waddled across the room and grabbed a bagpipe from a hook on the wall. He tapped, pumped, and blew on the pipes. Soon the instrument began to whine.

Lucas stuck his fingers in his ears.
"Too earsplitting!" he declared.

Master Aldrich set down the bagpipes, cleared his throat, and adjusted his glasses.

"How can you hope to master a

kingdom if you can't master some-thing as simple as a musical instru-ment?" he said.

Lucas shrugged again.

"Music brings joy and happiness!" his teacher said excitedly. "It brings kingdoms together. It can even save lives!"

Save lives? Master Aldrich sounded a little bit loopy to Lucas.

I'd better pick an instrument to get him to stop talking, he thought.

He settled on a stringed instrument with a long neck and a body shaped like pear sliced lengthwise.

"Ah, splendid, my prince!" said Master Aldrich. "You've chosen the lute! It will take years of hard work to master, but the reward for playing beautiful music is priceless!"

Oh no, thought Lucas. *Years of hard work to master?*

What had the prince gotten himself into this time?

CHAPTER 2

The Feather

The next day Lucas and Clara went berry picking on Primlox, the island of fairies. The fairies grew the sweetest fruit in the kingdom of Wrenly. Clara filled her bucket to the top with black raspberries.

"How many have you got?" asked Clara.

Lucas wiped his mouth with the back of his hand. His fingers and mouth had purple berry stains.

Clara shook her head. "Did you collect *any*?" she cried.

Lucas blushed. "A few," he said sheepishly.

Clara peeked into his bucket. "Cook will need more berries

than *that* to make his pies," she said. "Let's pick some more, but we'd better hurry or you'll be late for your music lesson again."

Plink! Plink! Plink! Lucas and Clara picked berries and dropped them into his nearly empty bucket.

"Well, I don't care if I'm on time," said Lucas. "I hate music lessons."

Clara stopped picking and threw a berry at Lucas. It pinged his cheek and fell to the ground.

"Hey!" said Lucas, wiping his face clean of the berry stains.

"Do you want to get in trouble again?" Clara asked.

"No," said Lucas, flinging a berry back at his friend. "But I still don't want to take music lessons."

18

Just as an all-out berry war was starting, they heard a great flapping of wings. Ruskin, who had been napping in the crook of a nearby tree, began to growl. He jumped down from the tree and scampered into the underbrush.

"Ruskin!"
Lucas shouted.
He and Clara

left their buckets and raced after him. Ruskin stood on the other side of the thicket and squawked at the sky.

"That's strange," said Clara, studying the sky. "I don't see anything. Do you?"

"No," said Lucas. "But look at this!"

He pointed at the ground. There, at their feet, lay a magnificent emerald green feather with shimmering silver and gold speckles.

Lucas picked up the glittering feather and measured it against his arm. "It's longer than my forearm!" he said.

Clara ran her finger down the length of the feather. "It must have come from a very large bird."

They both studied the sky for more clues, but all they saw were dark clouds rolling in.

"Wait," said Lucas. "Listen. Do you hear that? What's that other sound?"

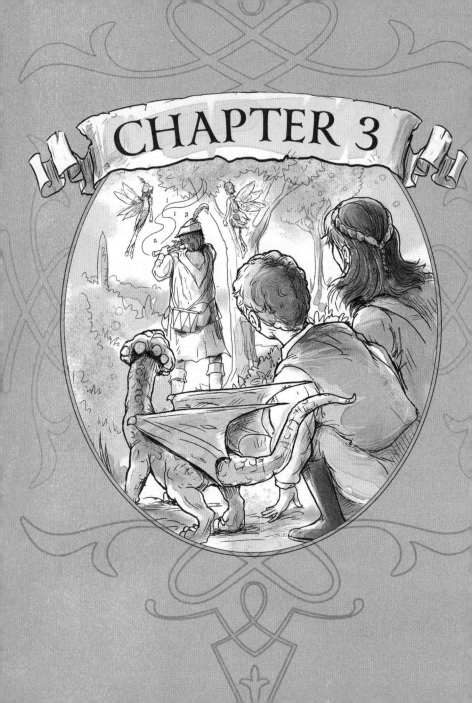

CHAPTER 3

The Bard

Clara stopped searching the sky for clues and listened.

Someone was playing a merry tune on a pipe nearby.

"It's coming from over there!" she said, pointing to another thicket of berry bushes.

The children crept quietly around the thicket and pulled back some branches. Ruskin burrowed under the brush to get a better look. There, in a clearing, stood a slender young man. He had chestnut brown hair tucked under a green felt hat. He wore a wool tunic and trousers, had a number of instruments hanging on straps from his belt, and had a guitar case by his feet. Two fairies

fluttered on
either side of him.

"It looks like a bard," whispered
Lucas.

A bard was a traveling musician.
Lucas had seen them come to Wrenly
before. They traveled throughout
kingdoms and played music in the
castles and inns along the way.

Clara nodded.

The bard played his pipe for a small bird in a tree above. Clara thought it might be a fairywren. The sandy-brown bird cocked her head as she listened to the music. Then she chirped and twittered the same tune back to the bard in response.

Ruskin let out a growl and leaped through the bramble. He bounded up to the man with the pipe and sniffed his trousers. The bard backed away uncomfortably. The fairies

buzzed around Ruskin's head and scolded him.

"Down, Ruskin!" Lucas called as he scrambled through the under-growth and into the clearing.

Ruskin grumbled but sat down.

"Stay," said the prince.

Ruskin stayed.

"Good boy."

Then Lucas noticed that one of the fairies was their friend Rainbow Frost. The fairy curtsied before the prince and introduced her friends.

"Prince Lucas, this is my sister, Amber Quill," Rainbow Frost said. "And this is our friend William, the wandering bard."

William took off his hat and bowed before the prince. His hair spilled over his face. "Pleased to meet you, Your Highness," he said. "Call me Will."

Then Lucas introduced Clara and Ruskin.

"Tell us, how did you get that fairywren to speak to you?" asked Clara.

Will lifted his pipe to his lips and

played a quick melody. "With music,"
he said. "I study all kinds of music—
even birdsong. I'm also in search of
another creature, who responds only
to music."

Clara looked at the fairywren in

the tree and then back at Will. "Do you actually know what that bird is saying?" she asked.

"In a way," said Will. "I've been listening to this mother fairywren for days. She's teaching her unhatched eggs a special song—one only her chicks will know."

Lucas spied the fairywren's nest
in the tree. "Why does she do that?"
he asked.

Will put his pipe in his pocket.
"So when her chicks ask for food,

she'll know it's her own children calling and not another animal who might be trying to trick her," he said.

"That's amazing!" Clara said.

"It is," Will agreed. "Music

has many unexpected uses."

Lucas suddenly clapped his hand over his mouth. "That reminds me!" he exclaimed. "We have to go, or I'll be late for my music lesson—*again!*"

CHAPTER 4

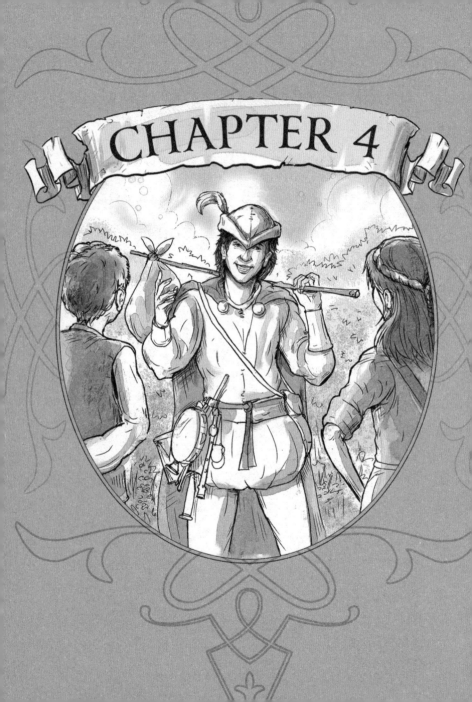

Our Guest

"May I join you?" asked Will. "I had planned to visit all of Wrenly and would much rather travel with you and Miss Clara than all by myself."

"Of course," Lucas answered. "But we need to leave right away."

"I'll gather my things!" the bard said cheerfully. He swung a bag over his shoulder and picked up his guitar case.

"I'll be right back," Lucas said.
"I have to get our buckets." He ran
toward the thicket.

"Hurry!" Clara exclaimed.

"I will!" said Lucas as he disappeared into the thicket, with
Ruskin close at his heels.

Lucas grabbed the berry buckets. Then he noticed the beautiful emerald green feather he'd dropped. He wondered again what kind of bird or beast it had come from. He slid the feather inside his vest and ran back to the others.

Rainbow Frost and Amber Quill waved good-bye to their friends at the dock. The ship set sail and rolled over the waves toward the mainland. Thunder rumbled and rain began to speckle the ground when they landed near the palace. Clara covered her head with a scarf and ran all the

way home. Will and Lucas tramped toward the castle in the light drizzle.

The queen greeted them at the door. She had been waiting.

"Lucas!" she cried. "You're late for your music lesson *again*!"

"If you'll excuse me, Your Majesty," Will said, bowing. "The prince is late because of me."

"And who might you be?" asked the queen.

Lucas introduced Will to his mother.

"Well then," said the queen, "I'll take care of our guest, and, Lucas, I want you to get to your lesson—*now.*"

The prince handed the berry buckets to Will and ran all the way to the music room.

At dinner Lucas glared at his
sore fingertips. They had dents from
pressing the strings on his lute. The
music lesson had been miserable. He
wanted to complain to his parents,
but that would only remind them

that he had been late to his lesson. Besides, his mother and father were more interested in their guest, Will, the wandering bard.

"Tell us, Will, where have you traveled recently?" asked King Caleb.

Will set a forkful of potato on his plate. "This trip has taken me to the kingdom of Bearwood, the Tower of Lyon, and the Fortress at Fenwick Falls. I've also traveled to Primlox, and now I am here in your fair palace.

No sooner than he said "fair palace," thunder boomed outside.

"Make that the stormy palace of Wrenly," the king said with a chuckle.

48

Will laughed. Then he talked about his travels while they ate a meal of potatoes, roasted meat, fish, warm bread with a hearty soup, and black-raspberry pie for dessert.

"Would you like me to play some music?" asked Will as the plates were cleared.

"Very much!" said the king.

"Let's have tea and music in the great hall," the queen suggested.

"Will you tell us a story too?" asked Lucas.

"First we will have music! Then we'll have a story," Will said. "How's that?"

"Perfect!" said Lucas.

All the people in the

castle gathered to hear the music. Will sat in a chair in the middle with the floating harp. He played a song

about a faraway princess locked in a tower. Then he sang about a blacksmith's daughter, who was tough as iron. His voice was gentle and he played the harp like an angel. He also played his pipe and guitar.

"And now," said the bard, setting down his guitar, "I shall tell you 'The Tale of the Bard'!"

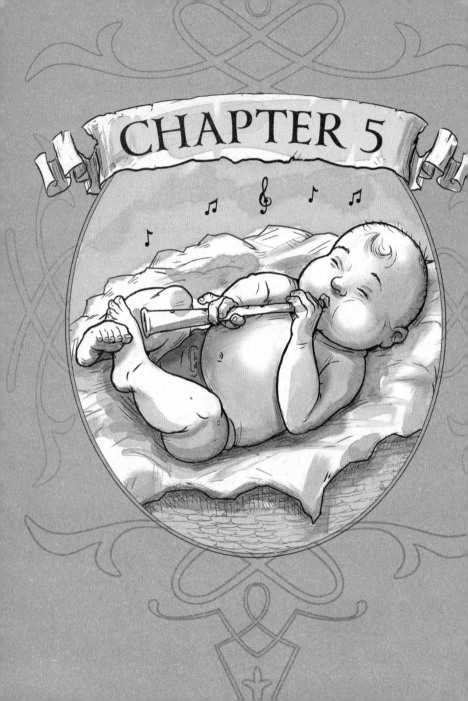

CHAPTER 5

The Bard's Tale

"Long ago, when I was a wee little bard, my mother misplaced my rattle. As I lay howling in my baby basket, she reached for the nearest thing she could find—a musical pipe. I grasped the pipe in my fist and put it straight into my mouth. From that day on, I played the pipe every day. I played for anyone and anything that would listen: cats, dogs, and

field mice—even garden snakes. I
discovered I could get animals to
follow me just by playing music!

"When I grew up, King Ashwin of
Meadowlark made me the minister

of pest control. I led the kingdom's
rats and snakes away with music.
All was well until a deadly pest was
found in the kingdom. It happened
like this:

"King Ashwin loved to fish. Every weekend, he fished on the Snake River, a river that squiggled across the countryside like its slithering namesake. There had long been a legend of an enormous beast that lived in the winding river, but nobody was sure if it was really true.

"One afternoon at dusk, the king and Sir Gavin, his closest companion, paddled home after a day of fishing. As they glided along, a huge snake swam up to the boat and lifted its head above the water. King Ashwin yelped in horror! He lifted his paddle and whacked the snake on its head. The snake bared its fangs and rose higher to attack them. It towered over the little boat. Sir Gavin waved his hands to confuse the creature. It shook its head wildly and then lowered itself into the water and disappeared.

"The king and his friend paddled to shore and hurried back to the palace. Little did they know, the snake watched from the river's edge. That night, the snake slithered through the farmers' fields. It glided across the schoolyard and through the village. The castle guards saw the serpent coming and summoned Sir Gavin and the knights.

"'It's too big for the knights!' Sir Gavin exclaimed. 'It must be more than a hundred feet long! And six feet wide! There is only one way to stop this savage beast.'

"That was when Sir Gavin summoned me. And it was just in time too. For when we entered the king's sleeping chambers, I gasped at the sight! The giant snake stood over the king with its jaws wide open. He was about to swallow the king whole! I lifted my pipe to my lips and played. The snake turned its evil red eyes on me. I played on. The snake began to listen. Its jaw relaxed and its face became dreamy. Soon the snake was in a trance. The king was safe."

Then the bard placed his hat over his heart.

"Thanks to music, all was well once again in the kingdom of Meadowlark. To this day, I still search for beasts that can be tamed with music, which is why I have come to Wrenly."

The castle crowd stood up and clapped and whistled for the bard.

Well, he won't find any beasts in Wrenly, thought Lucas. *But at least I can offer to show him around.*

CHAPTER 6

Substitute Teacher

Lucas lay in bed and listened to the birds chirp happily along the castle wall. *I wonder if Will's up?* he thought. The prince hopped out of bed, changed his clothes, and ran down the spiral stone staircase to the dining room. Will and the king were already having breakfast.

"Good morning, Will," said the prince. "How would you like me to

show you more of Wrenly today?"

"I'd like that very much," Will replied. "I had planned to do some exploring."

The king smiled. "What a wonderful idea!" he said.

"It is a nice idea," said the queen,

who had just entered the room, "but I'm afraid Lucas can't go. He has a music lesson today."

Lucas's fork clattered onto his plate.

"It's not like the lesson takes the *whole* day," he complained.

"True," said his father. "But you've been late for your first two lessons."

"But this is *special*," Lucas argued. "Will has never been to

Wrenly before, and who knows when he'll be back?"

The king shook his head and sighed.

"Your Majesties, if you'll excuse me," said Will, "I have an idea."

The king raised his eyebrows.

"Well, let us hear it," he said.

"What if *I* give Lucas his music lesson today? We could have it outside on the palace grounds."

The king looked to his wife. She nodded approvingly.

"It's a perfect solution," she said. "I'll let Lucas's music teacher know that the prince has a special guest teacher today."

"What do you say, Lucas?" asked Will.

"I'll do it!" replied the prince. He would rather be outside with Will—even if it meant he still had to have a music lesson.

"Now, don't forget your lute," his father said with a wink.

Lucas rolled his eyes. "I'll do my best to remember it," he said.

CHAPTER 7

A Lullaby

Lucas slung the lute across his back with a leather strap. Then he showed Will around the palace gardens. Ruskin followed close behind, sniffing shrubs and snapping at a low-flying dragonfly. Will told more stories about how he had used his wooden pipe to lead knights into battle and to play wedding marches.

"In all my travels there is one

thing I know to be true," Will said.

"What's that?" asked Lucas.

Will looked at his pipe fondly and said, "Music matters."

Lucas sighed. "I wish it mattered to me," he said glumly.

Will tousled Lucas's hair and laughed. "You have to give it a chance," he said. Then he sat down on a stone bench and motioned for Lucas to join him.

"Let's have that lesson I promised you," Will said.

Lucas did not want to play music, but he pulled out the lute.

"Now hand it over," Will said with a wink.

Lucas handed his lute to the bard.

"I'm going to teach you a very simple lullaby," he said. "There are only three chords. Watch carefully."

Lucas watched the bard play

the lullaby. He used the same three chords the prince had learned the day before.

"Now it's your turn," said the bard.

Lucas held the lute, and Will reminded him how to press his fingers on the strings next to the frets, the little wooden ridges on the fingerboard. Lucas strummed the first chord.

"It sounds like a sick fly," he said.

Will smiled. "Be patient. You'll get it."

Lucas tried again and again. The strings buzzed when his fingers weren't in the right spots. Ruskin lay down and put his claws over his ears.

"Not even Ruskin likes it," the prince said, "and he usually likes everything I do!"

Will tried not to laugh. "You're getting better every time," he said. "I think you'll be good enough to play for your parents tonight!"

"You have some high hopes," said Lucas.

They both laughed.

"Maybe we should give Ruskin a break?" suggested Lucas hopefully.

"Why not!" Will said with a smile.

Then they got up and strolled down a path and deeper into the woods.

CHAPTER 8

The Cave

Shafts of sunlight shined through the leafy treetops as they walked along the trail. They hiked beside a creek and up and down rolling hills. Ruskin bounded after squirrels and glided back to the boy and the bard.

Then Lucas stopped and pointed to a dark opening between two boulders. "Want to explore the cave?" he asked.

Will squinted at the dark cave. "Let's be careful," he said. "You never know what might be living in there."

Lucas laughed. "You don't need to worry about *this* cave," he said. "I've peeked inside lots of times, and nothing's ever been living in it. Well, maybe a few lizards."

Ruskin bounded toward the shadowy entrance, and Lucas followed. He wanted to show Will how brave he was. Near the mouth of the cave, Lucas noticed an emerald green feather on the ground. It looked just like the one he had found on

Primlox. He bent down and picked it up. Ruskin sniffed the feather, and then he sniffed the ground near the mouth of the cave. He cocked his head to the side. Something rustled deep inside the cave. Ruskin growled.

"What is it, boy?" Lucas asked. Before Ruskin could answer, a loud screech came from inside the cave.

"*Aiyeeee!*"

Ruskin yelped and ran back to Lucas.

"LUCAS!" shouted Will with great force. "SHUT YOUR EYES!"

Will spoke with such authority that Lucas dropped the feather and shut his eyes. Ruskin whimpered and closed his eyes too.

"Now what?" cried Lucas.

"Hold on!" shouted Will. "I'm coming! JUST DON'T LOOK!"

"WHAT IS IT?" asked Lucas, his heart pounding.

He wanted to run away, but he couldn't go anywhere with his eyes shut.

"*Aiyeeee!*" screeched the creature again.

"It's a basilisk!" Will shouted. "If

you look into its eyes, it will kill you!"

But the prince was itching with curiosity. Lucas shaded his eyes with one hand and peeked down at the ground. He saw a pair of enormous chicken feet. Suddenly Will clapped a hand over Lucas's eyes.

"Do not look!" repeated Will. "When I remove my hand, you must keep your eyes closed."

"Okay, okay!" Lucas said. "Then what?"

"Then we must play music," Will whispered.

"Excuse me? I don't think this monster is going to like my music any more than I do!" he cried.

"We're going put the basilisk to sleep with music," said Will. "It's our only chance."

Lucas could smell the creature's rotten fish breath.

"Okay, that's gross. Will, please *start playing*!" pleaded Lucas.

"I will!" said the bard. "But I'm going to need your help."

CHAPTER 9

A Duet

"What do you mean, you need *my* help?" Lucas asked.

"*Aiyeeee!*" The creature screeched again.

Lucas squirmed uncomfortably.

"Hold still," Will said. "We're going to play the lullaby I just taught you."

"But I can barely play it with my eyes open!" Lucas complained.

"You can do it," said Will calmly. "Now get your lute in position."

Lucas knew he had no choice. Their lives depended on it. "Okay," he said reluctantly.

Will lifted his hands from Lucas's eyes. The prince quickly swung his lute into place. Will grabbed his pipe.

The beast's claws scratched the ground as it slowly came closer. Lucas gulped.

"Don't think too much," Will said. "Just play the chords."

Lucas put his fingers in place. A bead of sweat rolled down the side of his face.

Will began to play the lullaby on his pipe. The gentle notes calmed Lucas down. He took a deep breath and strummed along on his lute. They played the whole lullaby. Lucas didn't make a single mistake. Then they sat still and listened. It had become very quiet.

Will nudged Lucas. "You can open your eyes," he whispered. "It's safe."

Lucas slowly opened his eyes and gasped. There, on the ground before them, lay a very strange creature.

It sort of looked like a rooster, except
for its monstrous size—and serpent's
tail. It had emerald green feathers
with shimmering silver and gold
speckles—like the one Lucas had

found on Primlox. The creature was fast asleep.

"So that's a basilisk," said Lucas as he gaped at the beast. He had only seen them painted in books of fairy tales.

"It is," said Will. "And our song should keep the beast asleep long enough for us to find help. Still, we must hurry." He turned toward the trail. "Come on. Let's go!" he whispered.

Lucas and Ruskin tiptoed
as fast as they could after Will.
They didn't speak another word
until they had reached the castle.

CHAPTER 10

Promises

Lucas and Will burst into the library, with Ruskin in tow.

"Father!" shouted Lucas. "You are never going to believe what happened!"

The king and queen had been discussing castle improvements with Stefan, one of the king's men. They turned to see what was going on.

"Slow down, Lucas!" his father

said. "Why don't you and Will have a seat and tell us your news?"

Lucas and Will sat down.

"What in the world has you two so wide-eyed?" asked the queen from a nearby couch.

Lucas looked at Will.

"We stumbled upon the beast I've been hunting for years!" Will said. "We found a basilisk!"

"You *what*?" questioned the king.

Lucas explained how they'd come across the basilisk in the woods.

"We've never had anything like that in the kingdom before," said the king. "Do you know how dangerous they are?"

"Yes, Your Majesty," said Will. "They're deadly creatures."

"And where is it now?" asked the king.

"The beast is asleep in the woods," Will said. "Please, you must hurry."

The king turned to Stefan. "Please send a message to André and Grom at once! Those wizards will know

how to handle a basilisk. We will find
a safe home for the poor creature, I
promise."

Then the king turned his attention back to Will and Lucas. "You two are lucky to be alive," said the king. "How did you do it?"

Lucas smiled proudly. "Believe it or not, music saved us," he said.

The king wrinkled his brow. "In the same way Will charmed the snake?" he asked.

"Exactly," said the bard. "Let us show you."

The king nodded eagerly.

The prince grabbed his lute and carefully positioned his fingers. Then the bard and the boy played the

lullaby. The king and queen clapped loudly once they had finished.

"Bravo!" said the king.

"Well done!" added the queen.

Then Will tapped Lucas on the shoulder with his pipe. "So, how do you feel about music now?" asked the bard.

Lucas thought for a moment. "I

feel thankful," he said. "I never knew music had so many uses."

Will patted the prince on the back. "You're a good student," he said.

Lucas smiled proudly. Then he had a sudden idea. "Will *you* be my teacher from now on?" asked the prince.

Will sighed. "I wish I could, but wandering bards must explore new lands," he said. "I have creatures to hunt and kingdoms to save!"

Lucas hung his head, though he wasn't surprised. "Will you come back and visit us?" he asked.

"Someday," said Will, putting his arm around Lucas.

"And will you tell us more stories?" asked the prince.

"I promise," said the bard. "But you must play your lute for me."

Lucas grinned. "Deal!" he said.

Hear ye! Hear ye!
Presenting the next book from
The Kingdom of Wrenly!
Here's a sneak peek!

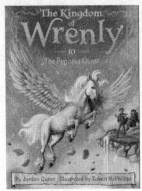

Prince Lucas and his best friend, Clara Gills, leaned on the balcony railing and gazed at the full moon. A ribbon of blue light shimmered across the Sea of Wrenly. But this was no ordinary moon. It was a *blue* moon—something so rare it happened only once in a lifetime. King Caleb said all the owls in the kingdom flocked together and sang once

Excerpt from *The Pegasus Quest*

in a blue moon. Lucas and Clara waited and listened for the owl song.

Ruskin yawned and curled up near the children. The young scarlet dragon had no interest in singing owls. He shut his eyes and sighed peacefully.

"Look at that enormous blue cloud," said Clara, pointing.

Lucas tilted his head back. "It's been there since this afternoon," he said.

"I know," Clara said, studying the cloud. "It hasn't budged."

Lucas looked at the great cloud

Excerpt from *The Pegasus Quest*

thoughtfully. "Maybe there's a floating castle inside it," he said.

Clara laughed. "You read too many fairy tales!" she said jokingly.

"And most of them have turned out to be true," Lucas reminded her.

Clara shook her head. "You're such a dreamer."

Then they began to hear a steady thrum. It sounded like the deep beating of wings. The friends turned toward the blue moon and gasped in wonder. Hundreds of owls swirled across the moonlight.

Excerpt from *The Pegasus Quest*